INTERIM

LOPEZ

Dedication

For those who lingered in the in-between

You were never alone.

First Edition published 2025

Second Edition (Revised) 2026

Published by Veiled Truths Press

Printed in the United States of America

ISBN: 979-8-9937359-1-7

Thelopezbooks.com

Contents

Chapter One

"Ah—my head hurts."

The thought didn't echo. It didn't even sound like sound. Just words, disjointed and hollow, bouncing around inside his skull. He tried to stand, but his legs gave out. The floor caught him— cold, hard, too smooth to be real. He sat upright, blinking. No doors. No windows. No shadows. Just white.

"Where the hell am I?"

Silence answered. Not the peaceful kind, but the thick kind— like being underwater, but without the sound of water. No hum. No buzz. No breath. Just the vacuum.

Then came the ring—that high, glassy tone in his ears. The kind that creeps in when quiet lasts too long. It pulsed once. Then disappeared.

This wasn't normal silence. It had weight. Not on his skin—on his mind. Like pressure behind the eyes. Like a scream too old to make a sound.

He closed his eyes. Think. Think.

Where was I before this?

Blank.

Maybe he'd been driving. Or walking. Or... talking to someone?

Nothing. Like the thread had been cut. No last location. No lead-up. No moment of impact. Just... here.

He opened his eyes again. Same room. Same cold. Same quiet.

He was trying to retrace a path that didn't exist.

Come on. Think.

There had to be something before this. A hallway? A street? A face?

Nothing.

No time. No sense of how long he'd been here—minutes? Hours? Days?

He pressed his palms to his head, fingers digging into his scalp.

Focus.

Still nothing.

Then the silence thickened.

Not louder—heavier.

The pressure in his skull bloomed like static behind the eyes. That high-pitched ring returned, sharper now, knifing through the quiet like a warning. Then gone again.

His breathing quickened.

Was he breathing? He couldn't hear it. Couldn't feel it.

He looked down. Chest rising? Falling?

He shot to his feet. Stumbled. Caught the wall—except it wasn't a wall. It was just... more—white. No seam. No edge. Just surface.

His heart started pounding. Or maybe it wasn't. Maybe it was just the idea of a heartbeat—because if he put his hand to his chest, he wasn't sure he'd feel a thing.

"HELLO?!"

His voice cracked—but even that felt like a thought, not a sound. No echo. No bounce. Just nothing.

He backed away.

Pacing now.

Breath sharp. Movements jerky. Hands shaking.

The silence wrapped around him like a vacuum-sealed bag, tightening, squeezing, pressing.

What is this place? What is this place?

He couldn't think. Couldn't remember. Couldn't BREATHE.

The floor tilted—maybe. Or he did.

His legs gave out again, and this time he didn't catch himself.

He curled in on himself, hands over ears, rocking.

Nothing. Nothing. Nothing.

The pressure in his skull was unbearable now—like his mind was trying to split open to escape. The ringing returned, piercing this time, high pitched, sharp enough to feel like scratching behind his eyes. He clenched his jaw, grinding his teeth, the sound stabbing deeper and deeper, until it was the only thing left.

No air.

He tried to breathe.

Chest—tight.

Throat—closed.

No breath.

No sound.

Just the ring.

His limbs twitched. Vision blurred. The room distorted, stretching at the edges. Or maybe that was him, slipping.

Please…

And then—nothing.

He blacked out, falling not forward, not back… but inward.

Chapter Two

He opened his eyes.

Same room. Same white.

But something felt… thinner. Like the silence had been stretched too far and might snap.

He didn't panic this time. Not yet. He just lay there, blinking slowly, trying to feel his own breath.

Still nothing. No sound. No warmth. Just the idea of lungs working.

He pushed himself upright, slower than before. Every movement carried the weight of déjà vu.

Was this the same spot he'd blacked out in? Or did the room shift while he slept?

No way to know.

The room gave nothing.

He stood. Legs shaky, but they held.

The surface beneath his feet felt less like a floor and more like… presence.

It didn't echo. Didn't creak. Just existed, the way a dream exists—there, until it isn't.

He walked the perimeter.

Five steps. Turn.

Six steps. Turn.

No seams. No shadows. No marks.

He tried to make sense of the space. Build a map in his head. But every time he turned, it felt like the room rewrote itself behind his back.

And then he saw it.

A bed.

Across the room. Dead center against the far wall.

It hadn't been there. He was sure of it.

Not because he remembered, but because something in his bones recoiled at the sight of it.

It was too clean.

Four rigid legs. Flat boards. A thin mattress with a tight white sheet pulled over it.

No pillow. No indent. No invitation.

It looked like it had been assembled, not placed. As if someone had slid pieces into slots and left before he noticed.

He froze.

He turned around slowly, looking behind him. Nothing.

Turned back.

The bed remained.

He approached it in careful steps.

9

There was no smell. No dust. No fibers in the sheet. It was sterile—aggressively sterile, like it had never been touched by skin.

He reached out, touched the frame. It was cold.

He circled it once, keeping a hand on the wood to remind himself it was real.

No drawer. No blanket. Just an object. A presence. A suggestion.

His mouth felt dry.

"Is this mine?" he whispered.

The room swallowed the words.

He stood there a moment longer, staring. Trying to catch it… doing something.

Shifting. Flickering.

But the bed just existed, like it always had—even if it hadn't.

He stepped back.

Two paces.

Three.

Stopped.

Turned away. Faced the blank wall across from it.

Took a breath. Or thought he did.

Turned back.

The bed was gone.

Nothing in its place.

Just a smooth floor, as if it had never been there.

Except... a faint crease ran across the surface—like the memory of weight.

Not an object. An impression.

He backed away slowly. He didn't trust the room. Didn't trust his own eyes.

But what other options were there?

He ran a hand through his hair. Fingers trembled slightly.

"Alright," he muttered. "Alright."

Think.

What does this mean?

The room was responding. That was the only explanation. It was alive—not with thoughts, but with something else.

It mirrored him. Or mocked him. Or maybe it didn't care at all.

He looked down at his hands.

They were steady now.

He clenched and unclenched them, testing the sensation.

No pain. No warmth.

He said his name.

Or tried to.

It caught in his throat—not from fear, but from emptiness. Like reaching for a tool that wasn't there.

He didn't know his name.

The thought slid past his defenses and sat heavily in his chest.

No name. No past. No voice. Just this.

This room.

This silence.

He turned and pressed his back to the wall. Slowly slid down until he was sitting again.

He stared across the room, breathing shallow. He counted each inhale, each exhale—even if he couldn't feel them.

The floor in front of him was blank. Unmarked.

Until it wasn't.

There, about ten feet away, sat a wooden chair.

Simple. Pale. Unfinished. No cushion.

Slatted back. Worn edges.

It looked… familiar.

Not in the way the bed had startled him. This felt different.

It didn't feel placed.

It felt remembered.

He stared at it, frozen.

A chair like that sat in his kitchen.

That was the thought—unbidden. Clear. Strong.

A memory, maybe. Or the echo of one.

He opened his mouth.

No words came.

The silence pressed in around him, but for the first time, it didn't feel empty.

It felt… patient.

Watching.

Waiting.

Chapter Three

He didn't mean to fall asleep.

One blink too long. Then another.
And then the weight behind his eyes won.

He sat against the wall, arms loose at his sides, the wooden chair still across from him. Unmoved. Unmoving. Just there.

His head tilted. Chin touched chest.

Stillness.

Then—slippage.

Not a fall, not a drift. Just… a tilt. Like the floor itself leaned, and he slid softly into something underneath it.

The silence changed.

It thickened, like fog. Then thinned. Then bloomed again with a low, throbbing hum.

He floated. Or maybe he walked. His limbs responded, but not well.

Everything was syrup. Weight clung to every muscle.

He opened his eyes, or thought he did.

There was a table.

A window?

Light spilled in from somewhere overhead, pale and slanted.

He reached out to touch the edge of the table, but his fingers took seconds to move.

Voices.

Muffled. Indistinct.

They pressed into his ears like cotton.

One soft.

One deep.

A rhythm between them — too fast to follow, too low to understand. Like listening through a wall with water in your ears.

He turned his head toward them.

Slow. Straining.

Shadows moved in the corner of the room.

A shape passed in front of the light.

Maybe a woman.

Maybe not.

He tried to call out. Nothing.

Another shape now. Sitting. Standing. Laughing?

Or was that crying?

He tried to squint. Tried to sharpen the image. But the world refused to hold still.

Every face blurred the second he tried to see it.

Every voice slipped into mud.

The air in this place tasted familiar.

Like bread and dust.

Like old carpet and open windows.

He knew this place. Knew the scent. Knew the feeling—but not the names. Not the people.
Just the edges of them.

A flicker—

Laughter.

A higher voice. A child?

Gone.

The room darkened at the edges. Something crawled into the periphery, sliding behind the walls of the dream.

He felt it before he saw it.

Wrong.

Heavy.

A shadow. Taller than the others. Not shaped like a person, but like the idea of one.

It didn't walk. It didn't move. It just… pressed.

He turned toward it.

It didn't fade.

He reached out—

And then—

BEEP.

One sharp, piercing note. Clean and unnatural.

And then—

White.

He was upright. Eyes wide. Breath sharp.

The room.

The chair.

Back.

No memory of waking. No transition. No ramp-up. Just there.

He blinked. His shirt clung to his back—sweat.

The silence had returned. But it felt different. Not dead. Not flat.

Disturbed.

He glanced at the chair. Still where it was. Still plain, wooden, familiar.

His breathing slowed. Or maybe it didn't.
He still couldn't hear it.

He rubbed his palms against the floor. It was cold again.

Smooth.

Untouched.

But his hands weren't steady.

He stared at his fingers like they belonged to someone else.

The dream—if that's what it was—lingered like a film behind his eyes.

He tried to recall the noise—the sound that had pulled him out.

Nothing.

No word for it. No echo. Just a hollow pause between what was and what is.

He looked down.

Whispered:

"I've been here before."

He wasn't sure if he meant the room.

Or the feeling.

And he didn't want to find out.

Chapter Four

He hadn't moved since waking.

The sweat on his back was starting to cool, drying into the fabric of his shirt. His arms were folded loosely across his chest, legs drawn in just enough to keep tension in his thighs. Not fear. Just… readiness.

The chair sat across from him.

Still.

Wooden.

Unchanged.

Except he wasn't sure it hadn't moved.

Just slightly.

Just enough.

He stood, slow. Careful. Like rising from prayer.

His bare feet pressed silently into the floor as he approached.

The light didn't change, but it felt dimmer now. Or maybe the air was thicker. Or maybe the silence was heavier.

He circled the chair.

Once.

Then again.

Each pass a little slower than the last.

It didn't feel threatening.

But it didn't feel right, either.

He stopped behind it, resting one hand on his chin, the other on his hip, leaning slightly.

It was a simple chair—plain slats for a back, rounded legs, seat smoothed from what looked like years of use. The kind of thing you'd find in an old house where nothing new had been bought in a decade.

Familiar. But not in a way he could place.

He bent down, brought his face near the wood.

Studied the grain.

Lines curved like old rivers.

A small knot twisted near one leg.

There were faint scratches—fingernail marks? Dragging lines? Nothing intentional, but not accidental either.

He reached out and touched it—barely. Just a fingertip on the top rail.

It felt like wood.

He slid his finger down the edge of the backrest, following the grain. Then along the seat's front edge.

Paused.

Pressed with his palm.

It was… warm?

Not hot. Not cold. But warm the way wood gets when it remembers the sun.

He curled his knuckles and tapped the side once.

The sound was small. Dull.

Not echoing—just present.

A sound that didn't carry, didn't ask to be remembered.

He tapped again, slower.

Felt the vibration trail up into his wrist.

The kind of sound you don't hear with your ears, but with your memory.

He sat.

Not suddenly.

He let his weight down as if testing whether the chair would allow it.

It didn't creak.

Didn't shift.

Just… held him.

His hands rested on his knees.

He waited.

The silence remained, but something inside it changed.

He didn't hear it. He felt it.

Like a shift in pressure behind the ears before a storm.

Like someone breathing in a dark room when you thought you were alone.

His eyes drifted to the far wall. Blank. Pale.

The space behind him grew colder.

Not the whole room.

Just behind.

Just enough for his skin to know it.

He turned his head slowly.

Nothing.

But his spine tingled.

His shoulders drew in.

There was no sound.

No flicker of movement.

But something was there.

Not in the room.

In the space around it.

The in-between.

He opened his mouth. Licked his lips.

"What do you want?" he said softly.

The question vanished into the stillness.

But something inside him shifted—not around him, within him.

Like a ripple in his chest.

And then… stillness again.

Chapter Five

The room was quiet again.

Not peaceful—never peaceful. Just… still.

He sat on the chair, elbows on his knees, staring at the far wall as if it might blink. The presence he'd felt before—cold, close, unseen—was gone now. Or at least, it was pretending to be.

"This isn't a room," he said softly. "It's… something else."

The words fell dead as they always did. No echo. No reply.

He took a breath. Or tried to.

Then pushed himself up.

The chair didn't creak. Just released him, like it had been waiting for him to leave.

He walked.

Not pacing, not panicking—just… moving.

The sound of his bare feet on the floor was more memory than noise.

He counted steps. Eight. Turn. Seven. Turn.

Nothing to mark the walls. No edges. No seams.

He stopped.

Closed his eyes.

"Okay," he whispered. "Think."

A name?

Nothing.

Birthday?

Nothing.

What about the last thing he ate?

His lips parted.

He almost said something.

Then it slipped.

He exhaled through his nose and pressed his palms to his temples.

His head didn't hurt—but it felt like it should.

He clenched his fists.

Harder.

Harder still.

Then it came.

A flicker.

Not an image. Not yet. Just a texture. Cold metal. A handle.

His eyes opened.

He saw it.

His hand—gripping a car door.

Rain tapping on the window.

And a voice—soft, familiar, saying:

"We're late."

Gone.

He gasped. Looked down at his hand.

Nothing in it.

He turned, scanned the white room. It hadn't changed.

But his chest felt tight.

"We?" he repeated, barely audible.

He said it again.

Louder.

"Who's we?"

No answer.

He began walking again, faster now.

Trying to force the memory to come back.

32

Another flash.

Warm light.

Hallway.

Muted voices.

Someone's face turned toward him—but blurred before he could see the eyes.

A mirror on the wall.

A reflection… but not of him.

Gone.

He stopped moving, grabbed at the wall like it might steady him.

The surface was still smooth.

He pounded a fist against it.

Harder.

Again.

Nothing. No sound. No pain.

But in his head, he heard the thump.

"I was there," he whispered.

Another fragment. A smell—burnt toast.

A plate on a table.

His hand reaching for it. A laugh. A woman's laugh?

He pressed both palms flat against the wall.

"Come on. Come on…"

The wall shifted.

Just for a second.

Not visually—tactilely. The texture beneath his hands changed.
Ridges. Grain.

Wood.

He gasped and stepped back.

The surface returned to smooth.

He stared at his hands.

They trembled slightly.

That... hadn't been imagined.

He looked around.

The chair was still there, behind him now.

The silence returned to its full weight.

His voice cracked as he said, "What are you trying to show me?"

Nothing.

He dropped to the floor, knees hitting harder than expected.

Elbows on thighs. Hands on his face.

Breath short.

And then—

A voice.

Not here.

Not in the room.

But not in his head either.

Not words exactly.

A phrase, like fog. Like wind through an open door.

"Wait for me."

Soft. Not pleading—promising. Like a rope thrown out to someone slipping away.

His hands dropped.

He looked up.

"Wait…" he whispered. "Wait for… who?"

The silence pressed in again.

But the pressure in his chest remained.

A tension that wasn't fear.

Something closer to… loss.

He looked to the far wall.

No crack.

No mark.

No proof.

Just a phrase, echoing in a place where echoes didn't exist.

Chapter Six

The silence had changed.

It wasn't stillness anymore.

It was waiting.

He sat against the wall where he'd first heard it—wait for me—but now it felt further away. Like whatever had reached out was slipping back through the cracks.

He stood. Slowly. His body still felt like his, but lighter, like the floor didn't push up as hard anymore.

"This isn't a room," he whispered. "It's something else."

He took a step forward.

The light overhead flickered.

Not a bulb. Not power. Something else.

Like the entire scene had reset for a frame.

And for a second, the walls shimmered—not with color, but with distortion, like glass trying to remember its shape.

He looked toward the far wall.

Something rippled there. Briefly.

Then gone.

He turned a slow circle.

The corners of the room were off now—slightly rounded, like the geometry had been misaligned.

His heart was steady, but his breath shortened.

Or maybe it was the air itself.

It was thinner now. Cooler. Then hot. Then cold again.

The silence cracked.

A sound cut through it.

Not in his head.

From outside.

A voice.

Soft. Urgent.

Feminine.

"Don't go…"

His entire body snapped toward it.

His knees locked. Hands clenched.

He stared into the wall it had come from—if it had come from anywhere.

"…Hello?"

Nothing.

He took a step forward.

Then another.

Faster now.

"HEY! I heard you—where are you?!"

The wall didn't move.

Didn't answer.

His voice rose.

"WHAT DO YOU MEAN DON'T GO?! WHO ARE YOU?!"

He slammed both fists against the wall.

"HELLO?! CAN YOU HEAR ME?!"

The floor shivered beneath his feet.

Not a quake—just a breath.

He backed up. Looked down.

Then around.

The light overhead pulsed once.

A slow strobe. Then steadied.

He turned in a circle again.

No change.

But he felt it.

Something had shifted.

The wall across from him now bore a thin fracture.

Hairline. Vertical.

Like glass under pressure.

He stepped closer.

As he reached for it—

it vanished.

The wall was smooth again.

He stood still. Stared at his hand.

His palm tingled. Numbness, then pins.

He didn't know if it was from the wall or the fear.

He turned slowly, looking for the chair.

Gone.

No sound. No movement. Just gone.

It was like it had never been there.

"Say something," he said.

His voice was low now. Fragile.

"Please… say something else."

No reply.

But inside him—somewhere deeper than his thoughts—a voice moved.

Not external. Not memory.

Just… presence.

It didn't come through his ears.
It came through his chest.

A whisper.

Still here.

He froze.

His mouth stayed open a second too long.
Then closed.

He didn't know if it was his own thought, or someone else's.

He didn't know if it was a trick of the room.

Or something real trying to reach back.

He walked forward until he reached the wall where the fracture had been.

It looked the same.

But the air around it had changed.

He reached out.

Pressed his hand flat.

Warm.

Not ambient. Not body heat.

The wall itself was warmer than it should be.

He let his hand stay there.

"I'm still here," he said.

The room didn't respond.

But it didn't feel as empty as before.

Chapter Seven

He stood with his palm still resting against the warm wall.

The heat hadn't faded. But it hadn't grown either. Just held steady, like a body that wasn't his.

He pulled his hand away. Let it fall to his side.

Time didn't move here—not forward, not back. But something had shifted, and he felt it.

He stepped backward until the wall was no longer in reach, then turned slowly in place, taking in the room like a man surveying a battlefield.

"What do I know for sure?" he said aloud.

The silence listened.

He raised a finger with each point, voice low, steady. A quiet list made for himself—because there was no one else to hear it.

"One... the room changes."

"Two... things appear when I remember them."

"Three... they disappear when I don't."

"Four... voices come from outside."

He paused.

"Five... I'm not alone."

His hand dropped.

The air felt tighter now, like the pressure had increased by just a few degrees.

He started walking again—slow, controlled steps. Not pacing this time. Tracking.

He was halfway across the room when he saw it.

The chair.

Back again. But changed.

It wasn't in the center anymore.

It had moved to the right, near the wall where the crack had been.

And it wasn't facing outward.

It was turned—toward the wall. Slightly off-angle. Like someone had been sitting there, watching.

His heart didn't race.

It didn't need to.

He was past fear. Past panic.

He approached with deliberate steps, eyes fixed on the chair like it might flinch.

When he reached it, he didn't circle immediately.

He stood behind it.

Waited.

Then moved slowly, one foot at a time, around its side.

It looked the same.

But not.

There was a tension in the air around it—like heat clinging to skin before a thunderstorm.

He crouched.

Ran his fingers lightly along the backrest.

Same smooth grain.

Same slight warmth.

Then—

A scratch.

Low on the back. Diagonal. Jagged.

Not accidental.

He leaned in closer, brushing it with his thumb.

The wood had splintered slightly.

Too deep for a scrape.

Too focused to be random.

A single claw mark? A tool?

No. It didn't feel like an object did this.

It felt desperate.

Fingernails.

Someone had grabbed the back of the chair hard enough to dig in.

He sat on his heels, studying it.

"What happened to you?" he asked softly.

Then corrected himself.

"No… what happened here?"

He stood again and looked around the room.

Still blank.

Still white.

Still waiting.

But now the air vibrated.

Not sound. Not hum. Just resonance—like something alive had taken a breath on the other side of a wall.

His fingers traced the gouge again.

And the light overhead flickered once—soft, fast, almost like a blink.

He froze.

The flicker didn't come back.

But the temperature shifted.

The chair grew warmer beneath his touch.

He pulled his hand away, slowly.

Backed up two steps.

The room felt... reactive.

Alive.

He sat on the floor directly across from the chair.

Cross-legged.

Palms open on his knees.

Facing the thing like it might speak.

"If you're here…" he said quietly.

"…show me."

Nothing moved.

Nothing answered.

But the silence felt considered.

Like it wasn't ignoring him.

It was deciding.

Chapter Eight

He didn't move for a long time.

The room had gone still again, but not like before. Not hollow.

This stillness had depth. Like something had settled just beneath the surface and was waiting for him to notice.

He sat with his legs crossed, hands resting on his knees, eyes fixed on the chair.

It hadn't moved again.

Yet.

He let his eyes close—not to sleep, not to escape, but to listen.

Not for sound.

For whatever came next.

Then something shifted.

He smelled it.

Faint.

At first, he thought he imagined it.

Then stronger.

Toast.

Slightly burnt. Dry crust. Hints of melted butter and that warm, familiar edge that came not from food… but from routine.

His eyes opened.

He stood up slowly, breath shallow.

It wasn't random.

This wasn't just some recycled smell from a forgotten meal.

This was home.

He turned his head—slowly.

There, in the far corner of the room, stood a small wooden table.

It hadn't been there before.

Simple. Plain. The kind of table you'd never describe to someone because it wasn't special to anyone else.

But he knew it.

One leg slightly uneven. A small chip on the corner.

He'd hit his knee on that edge more times than he could count.

On the table sat a plate.

White. Cheap. Faded blue ring around the edge.

And on the plate:

A piece of toast.

Butter spread to the corners.

Edges dark—burnt, just slightly.

His chest tightened.

That toaster.

No matter the setting, it always did that.

He used to joke about it.

Or maybe she did.

He walked toward the table, each step lighter than the last.

When he reached it, he didn't touch it right away.

He just stared.

The toast was still warm.

He could smell the butter, the toast, the slight scorch from the edge.

His fingers hovered.

Then touched it.

Gone.

The table.

The plate.

The toast.

Gone.

As if they had never been there.

He stood frozen in place, hand still half-raised, like it was trying to remember what it was holding.

The scent lingered. Just for a moment.

Then faded.

He dropped to his knees. Hands flat on the floor.

"No… no, no, no."

He closed his eyes, pressed his forehead to the ground.

"Show me again," he whispered.

"I was there. I remember it. Show me again."

Nothing.

He clenched his fists. Pounded once.

Then again.

Silence.

"Please…"

He sat back. Breathing hard now.

That wasn't just memory.

That was real. For a moment.

He looked up—and froze.

The chair was gone.

He turned quickly—and saw it again.

Behind him.

Closer than before.

Facing him now.

Same scratch on the back.

The warmth had returned to the room.

But only in that spot.

He stared at the chair, unsure if he should move toward it again.

But his legs did the deciding.

One slow step. Then another.

He reached it.

Didn't touch it this time.

Just stood there, staring into the space it now faced.

What had it been watching?

What had been sitting in it?

He opened his mouth to speak, but something beat him to it.

A voice.

Soft. Distant.

"He's still in there."

His breath caught.

It hadn't come from inside.
It hadn't echoed in his skull.
It came from… beyond.

He turned toward the sound.

Too late.

Gone.
He stood there for a long time.
Not breathing.
Not thinking.

Just… listening.

Chapter Nine

The voice still echoed in his head.

He's still in there.

It hadn't spoken to him.

It had spoken about him.

And that made it worse.

He wasn't just alone.

He was observed.

He stood in the center of the room, fists curled at his sides.

The chair remained where it had last appeared—facing him, perfectly still.

He turned slowly, eyes sweeping the white space.

Something had changed. Not visibly, not fully.

But the room no longer felt endless.

There was a shape to it now.

Edges. Pressure.

He approached the far wall—where the table had once appeared.

Placed a hand against it.

Still smooth. Still cold.

But it trembled beneath his touch.

He leaned in, pressing harder.

The wall gave slightly.

Not like a door opening.

More like skin stretching.

Or vapor shifting around force.

He stepped forward.

And the world bent.

Not a flash. Not a fade.

Just—through.

The room was gone.

He was in a hallway.

Long. Narrow.

Just wide enough for one person.

Walls close, but not claustrophobic—just… specific.

As if it had been made for him.

The air was heavier here.

Cooler.

It smelled faintly of metal and dust.

A mechanical staleness.

The walls were gray—stained in places.

Blotches like old fingerprints.

Some looked like writing, but smeared, blurred, lost.

Overhead, long fluorescent lights stretched into the distance, buzzing faintly.

One flickered.

Another was out completely.

He turned to look behind him.

There was no door.

No threshold.

Just wall.

He was inside something now.

And whatever it was… it remembered him.

He walked slowly, feet making soft taps on the floor that finally echoed.

The first sound in what felt like forever.

Each footfall bounced back at him.

Not clean. Not sharp.

Delayed. Muted. Like the hallway had to think about how to respond.

The further he walked, the more certain he became:

This wasn't a room.

This wasn't a dream.

It was a memory—but not his.

Something shared. Or observed.

Halfway down the corridor, the air changed again.

Warmer.

Breath on the back of his neck.

He spun around.

Nothing there.

But he heard something ahead.

A faint sound.

Dripping.

Somewhere distant.

Water? Or something heavier?

He kept walking.

His fingers brushed along the wall.

It pulsed faintly under his skin—like a vein.

Like the entire place was alive.

Then he heard it.

Footsteps.

Not his.

Not echo.

Distinct. Behind him.

Slow. Measured.

He stopped.

The steps continued for another second.

Then silence.

He turned sharply.

Empty corridor.

He took two steps back.

Paused.

Waited.

Nothing.

But his heartbeat had quickened.

Or… the idea of it had.

Then a voice.

Faint. Behind the wall.

A woman's voice.

Familiar.

Crying.

Muffled. Gasping for breath between sobs.

He pressed his ear to the wall.

"Please… please…"

Then—cut off.

Like the scene ended.

He stepped back.

Face pale.

Lips parted.

This wasn't a mind.

This was a prison.

He turned forward.

And finally saw it.

At the end of the corridor—distant, small in the haze of flickering light—

A door.

Wooden.

Old.

Closed tight.

His breath caught.

He didn't hesitate.

He ran.

The corridor stretched as he moved, or maybe it just felt that way.

The walls blurred past him.

His footsteps rang louder now.

The sound returned to him fully.

The world was no longer silent.

The door grew larger with every stride.

His legs moved faster than they should have been able to.

He didn't tire.

He reached the door.

Raised his hand.

And just when he was about to reach for the handle...

Darkness.

Chapter Ten

Darkness.

Not the kind that lives behind closed eyes.

The kind that presses.

The kind that weighs.

He didn't remember falling.

Didn't remember blinking.

Just — standing one moment, reaching for the door,

and the next…

Nothing.

But he was awake.

Not dreaming.

Not moving.

Just… suspended.

He wasn't sure if he was standing or floating, only that the air felt thick, like water weighted down by ash.

He reached forward.

There was no forward.

Just black.

He tried to speak.

His voice didn't carry. It barely formed.

Then — a light.

No flash. No switch. Just… presence.

A faint gray outline of a room came into view.

The walls bowed outward slightly, like the space had been bent by pressure.

The floor beneath him pulsed with a faint, slow rhythm.

Like breath.

Like a heartbeat.

But not his.

And then he saw it.

The figure wasn't a figure.

It rose from the floor to the ceiling — a wall of shadow so black it made the dim light around it seem artificial.

It didn't move.

Didn't breathe.

But it took up space like a living thing.

At its base, thick mist poured across the floor in slow, curling waves — black like tar, but cold like dry ice. It flowed around his feet, too heavy to lift, too alive to ignore.

There was no face.

No limbs.

But it watched him.

He could feel its focus.

He didn't know how he knew, only that it looked down at him, and his chest tightened as if something inside him was shrinking away.

Not in fear.

In grief.

The air grew colder.

Not room-temperature cold — soul-cold.

Like being seen by something that remembers every time you've walked away.

He tried to speak.

Nothing.

His throat moved, but no sound escaped.

He stepped forward.

The mist pulled at his ankles.

The shadow remained still.

Then, without motion, it spoke.

It didn't use sound.

It used inside.

At first, he heard it in reverse—a series of breathy, distorted pulses that pressed inward like static.

Then clarity.

The voice turned forward.

Soft. Breath-heavy.

Feminine.

"Why did you leave me?"

He froze.

It wasn't accusation.

It wasn't anger.

It was hurt.

Deep. Old.

The kind of hurt that becomes shape.

He opened his mouth again, desperate to respond.

But his voice caught in his chest.

His lips moved, and the air did not.

The lights overhead flickered once.

Then steadied.

The shadow did not vanish.

It did not shrink.

But it stepped back.

Not physically—spiritually.

The pressure eased.

He dropped to one knee.

Hands on the floor.

Breath ragged, but still silent.

He didn't cry.

But he felt something crack.

Like a name had almost formed in his throat.

But not his.

Someone else's.

Someone he had left behind.

When he looked up again, the shadow was gone.

So was the mist.

The room remained dim, but somehow emptier than before.

The cold lingered in the bones of the place.

He stood slowly.

Turned a circle.

No door.

No corridor.

No chair.

Just the quiet.

But it wasn't watching him anymore.

Now…

it was waiting.

Chapter Eleven

It was still again.

But not the same kind of still.

This one felt… hollowed out.
Like the room had just exhaled everything it had.

He stood there, alone in the dim.

No chair.

No door.

No figure.

No light above.

Just him.

And the cold.

Not skin-deep — deeper. Like something had left with the shadow that had spoken.

He didn't feel afraid.

He felt unfinished.

Then he heard it.

Faint at first.

Not mechanical — more organic.

Like a heartbeat stretched into a long, low hum.

He turned toward the sound.

A faint glow formed ahead of him, right in the center of the floor.

It pulsed once.

Then again.

As he stepped closer, it began to shape itself — edges folding out of the dark, like paper pulled from water.

A machine.

A monitor.

Hospital-style, but softer. Faded. As if memory couldn't get the details quite right.

The screen glowed pale green.

Numbers blinked. A line pulsed slowly across the screen.

Then—

Text.

His name.

Spelled out plainly, without ceremony.

Jobe.

His knees nearly gave out.

He stared at it.

Not because he didn't believe it.

But because it felt like coming home to a face you forgot you missed.

He whispered it.

"...Jobe."

His own voice sounded new.

Like trying on something that had once belonged to someone else.

Then the air cracked.

No warning.

Just a sudden, vicious—

BANG.

Metal twisted somewhere out of sight.

A shriek of crunching steel.

Glass shattered behind him.

Then a distant siren, wailing through the dark like a scream underwater.

He spun in place, arms up, eyes wide.

The room split.

For a moment—just a moment—the space around him wasn't space anymore.

It was memory.

A hospital ceiling.

Harsh overhead lights.

A figure leaning over him—blurred, but clearly weeping.

A hand on his arm.

Tubes.

Voices—too many voices, all layered and panicked.

And then it was gone.

Like it had been pulled away before it could settle.

He gasped.

Dropped to his knees.

Hands braced against the ground, eyes shut tight.

"Stop… please stop…"

The room flickered again.

Static bled through the floor, the ceiling, the walls.

His name blinked on the monitor.

Jobe.

A voice followed.

Soft. Warm.

"Jobe… it's okay. We're right here."

He turned, fast, as if the voice had come from behind.

No one.
But it hadn't been a thought.
It hadn't been part of the room.

It was outside.

Real.

Alive.

Tears hit his cheeks before he realized he was crying.

The voice wasn't calling him back.

It was reminding him.

He was still in there.

He hadn't been forgotten.

He closed his eyes again, palms flat to the floor.

"I remember…" he whispered.

The floor vibrated once.

The monitor blinked.

And then everything went black.

Not like the lights had gone out.

Like the system had reset.

Chapter Twelve

Light.

Then dark.

Then light again.

A pulse.

Somewhere distant.

Not pain—just pressure, like his body was being pushed back into shape.

He tried to open his eyes.

Couldn't.

Tried again.

Everything flickered.

The white room.

A hospital ceiling.

Flickering fluorescent light.

A blurred figure leaning over him.

Gone.

Then came the sound.

The monitor.

Steady.

Then slower.

Slightly off-rhythm. Labored.

A voice, somewhere just outside him:

"His vitals are dropping."

Another voice—muffled, panicked:

"He's slipping again."

He tried to move.

His hand barely twitched.

Or maybe it didn't.

Maybe it was just the idea of movement, swimming inside a body that no longer obeyed.

He tried to speak.

His jaw clenched.

His breath stuck in his throat.

No sound.

The world glitched again.

The white room returned, pulsing softly at the edges, like breath behind glass.

But this time, it was blended—like layers of paint scraped together.

He saw the hospital room bleeding through the wall.

The silhouette of a woman.

Shoulders shaking.

Hand on his chest.

He reached for her.

But his arm didn't lift.

Not fully.

The floor beneath him buckled slightly.

Just a ripple.

Just enough to remind him this place wasn't real—not entirely.

The heartbeat slowed again.

Then skipped.

He heard it echo.

One long pause.

Then:

Beep.

...

...

Beep.

Weaker.

"I'm not ready," he whispered.

He didn't know if he meant to die.

Or to live.

He began crawling.

Not fast.

Not strong.

Just desperate.

One arm.

Then the next.

The floor rippled with every motion—thinning out like stretched plastic film.

The light above him dimmed.

Then flared.

Then dimmed again.

The hospital flashed again.

A woman's sob.

A hand brushing his face.

Then darkness again.

He kept crawling.

His fingers dragged lines behind him.

Not real marks—just impressions.

Memories.

Toast.

A chair.

A voice.

A name.

Jobe.

He stopped.

Rolled onto his back.

Stared into the shifting ceiling.

"I remember…"

He lifted his arm.

The monitor beeped again.

Slower.

Longer gaps.

Another voice—outside, faint, straining:

"Come on… please… come back…"

He reached toward it.

Up.

Up.

Like he could tear through the sky and climb out.

And just as his fingertips brushed the light—

Silence.

No heartbeat.

No breath.

No voices.

Just the cold, quiet weight of waiting.

Chapter Thirteen

Silence.

No flicker.

No motion.

No breath.

Just the flat, unblinking stillness of nothing.

He wasn't cold.

He wasn't warm.

He wasn't sure if he had a body anymore.

The air didn't hum.

The walls didn't pulse.

Even the white was gone.

Then—

Beep.

A single tone.

Long.

Steady.

Too steady.

Flatline.

Not in the room.

Outside.

He didn't hear it with his ears.

He felt it.

A sound, like a closing door.

Like someone saying goodbye through glass.

A voice.

Low. Faint. Distant.

"We're losing him…"

Another voice. Shaky. Weeping.

"No… not yet… please…"

He tried to speak.

Or move.

Or feel.

But there was no "he" to try with.

Only presence.

A shape suspended inside the pause between something and nothing.

Then—

a light.

Soft.

Not hospital bright.

Warm.

Like dawn through curtains.

Or childhood memory.

It pulsed once.

Then again.

His hand twitched.

Small. Barely visible.

Maybe a reflex.

Maybe a return.

Somewhere near the light—

a table.

Old.

Plain.

A chipped edge.

And on it:

Toast.

Slightly burnt.

Edges curled.

The scent drifted toward him.

And for a moment—

He was there.

All of him.

A voice—

"Time of death is…"

Silence.

Then—

"Wait. Did you see that?"

Another flicker.

His breath hitched.

A twitch at the corner of his mouth.

Or maybe a tremor in the light.

It was impossible to say.

The chair returned.

Facing him.

Still.

Empty.

Or waiting.

He reached forward.

Not fast.

Not frantic.

Just a hand rising slowly into the glow—

He didn't know if he was waking up… or letting go.

A Note From the Author

Interim was born from a question that's haunted me for a long time:

What if the space between life and death wasn't empty? What if it was… aware?

This story isn't about dying.

It's about memory.

About the weight of small routines.

About the ache of unfinished conversations and the smell of toast you didn't know you'd miss.

Jobe's journey is fictional, but the fear—the stillness, the wondering if someone's still "in there"—that's real.

For anyone who's ever sat beside a hospital bed, holding on, hoping for a sign:

This one's for you.

Whether Jobe woke up or let go… I'll leave that to you.

Thank you for reading.

— Lopez

About the Author

Lopez is a multidisciplinary creator whose work blends with gritty realism, philosophical undertones, and raw emotion. Being an entrepreneur, gunsmith, leather craftsman and writer, his storytelling spans fiction, design, and social commentary.

He is the founder of Veiled Truths Press and when not writing, you can find him customizing firearms, making leather goods, or working in his Southern California workshop.

Connect with him:

www.thelopezbooks.com

@kingdom05

Kingmagot.substack.com

Also by Lopez

Veiled Truths: The Lucian Graves Mysteries Vol's 1-3

A trilogy exploring secrets, survival, and the cost of clarity.

The Blood of the Son: A Cartel Family Saga

A story of the consequences of a sons decisions for the love of his father.

The Witnesses: The Fall of Eden

A cosmic reckoning that challenges the fate of humanity.

Find them at www.thelopezbooks.com

www.ingramcontent.com/pod-product-compliance
Lightning Source LLC
Chambersburg PA
CBHW012041140726
47991CB00011B/3225